To Mr. McCa

With radiating thanks

from Quump's Grandfather

D. A. Sampler

Grump and the Hairy Mammoth

DEREK SAMPSON

Grump and the Hairy Mammoth

Illustrated by Simon Stern

METHUEN CHILDREN'S BOOKS · LONDON

First published in Great Britain 1971
by Methuen Children's Books Ltd
11 New Fetter Lane, London EC4
Reprinted 1974
Text copyright © 1971 by Derek Sampson
Illustrations © 1971 by
Methuen Children's Books Ltd
Printed in Great Britain by
Whitstable Litho, Straker Brothers Ltd

ISBN 0 416 08370 6

Contents

I

Meet Grump

"Mashed potatoes, why am I so ugly!"

Grump sighed and kicked a stone with his bare toes. Life was hard for a caveman during the great Ice Age, so many thousands of years ago. None of the other Ice Age men were exactly pretty, but Grump was the strangest of all. His forehead was wrinkled like rumpled bedclothes, and his nose was scrunched up as if he could smell something awful. No wonder the other cavemen enjoyed pointing out how ugly he was.

"Well, if they don't like me, I don't like them!" Grump muttered. He glared at the men who stood chatting in the misty sunlight. "I can get along quite well alone."

It was true. Grump had long ago grown tired

of being teased, and learned to keep to himself. He had picked a leaky, draughty cave to live in, far from the rest of his tribe. He fed himself, walked by himself, talked to himself. But mainly he grumbled. That was why he was called Grump.

"What shall I do this morning? No need to look for food. I still have some tasty fruit from yesterday. What can I do instead?"

That was the worst of living in the Ice Age. It could be so boring. And all those melting, dripping glaciers were enough to drive Grump crazy.

"Got to find something to do," Grump grumbled, as he trudged up the hill above his cave. He was looking for mischief, and he wasn't long finding it. Suddenly he spotted something far below, under the cliff. He peered over the edge.

"What a surprise!" he chuckled. "It's old hairy horns, snoozing as usual."

From a patch of sunlight at the foot of the cliff came a snoring noise. It was made by a huge creature, sleeping in the warmth. Grump drew back hurriedly as the animal stirred.

"All right for him," he said. "All he has to do is eat a bit and sleep a bit. Nobody every bothers a mammoth."

That's what the sleeping animal was – a large hairy mammoth. Herman was his name, and he was the happiest creature alive. Perhaps that was what annoyed Grump about him. It didn't seem fair that anyone could be so cheerful. And what an easy life he had compared to Grump! No grubbing for roots to eat or crouching in the cold to catch a

coney rabbit. Herman just browsed happily off the tree tops, or slept warm and snug in his home-grown fur coat.

"Thinks he's got everything, doesn't he?" Grump complained. "So pleased with himself. If only I could take him down a peg or two!"

But how? Bouncing boulders on to Herman's head was useless. The mammoth would hardly notice. Grump needed something different. Suddenly he banged the earth in glee.

"Of course," he said. "I'll dig a nice big pit for catching mammoths in. Let's see how he likes that!"

Grump turned and scampered down the hill to a spot near Herman, but out of his sight. In a minute, he was at work, digging busily.

Chink! Chink! Chink! Herman lifted his head sleepily. What was that noise nearby? What was going on? He couldn't see anything. Wait! Something which looked like an old sack of paper, topped with a turnip, was flitting from rock to rock towards him. He recognized that figure of old. Grump was on the move again. Herman closed his eyes and pretended to sleep once more.

Grump was nervous. He had dug his pit, and covered it with giant ferns and dead branches. Now he had to make Herman chase him and fall into the pit. That would be the hard part. He shivered, and crept close to the snoring animal. Then he lifted one of the ears which lay in a great hairy flap over Herman's face.

"Silly old mammoth!" he shouted. "Your mother was a rug and your father was a hairy hallstand!"

Immediately he leaped away, terrified at what he had done. But Herman didn't move; not a stir, not a twitch. Suddenly an awful thought burst into Grump's brain. Was Herman sick, or even worse? And just when he'd worked so hard digging a lovely trap! It was too much to bear. With a cry of fury he jumped on to Herman's back and tugged at his furry coat.

"Wake up, bonehead! Wake up and chase me!"

That's where Grump made his mistake.

The moment he was on **Herman's** back, the mammoth heaved to his feet. With a toot of triumph, he started running, slowly at first then faster and faster. He meant no harm, of course. It was a game to him. But Grump was terrified.

Over rocks, over rivers, Herman ran. He darted through herds of dozing dinosaurs, slid down glaciers, lumbered over the lumpy landscape. But at last, even he began to tire. He headed back to their starting place.

Then he saw Grump's pit.

It was a very good pit, really, deep with straight sides, and the ferns hid it well. But Herman wasn't deceived. Just when he seemed sure to tumble in, he stopped suddenly. Grump sailed through the air, spinning like an acrobat, and landed on the ferns. He lay there for a second, then the ferns collapsed and he disappeared with a shout of despair.

"Oh! Ouch! I'm

shaken to shreds!" Grump grumbled as he picked himself up. He felt himself carefully. All his limbs seemed to be in place, just about. He looked up and saw Herman's big face staring down at him with interest, over the edge of the pit.

"Don't look so smug, flop ears," Grump bellowed, and waved his fist. "Just wait until I get out of here!"

The question was, how *could* he get out? The

pit was deep, very deep, big enough to hold the largest mammoth. How could a little caveman hope to escape? There was nothing to help him, unless you counted a few broken branches and withered ferns. Grump groaned and sat down. He was convinced by now it was all Herman's fault.

"What a thing to do to a nice harmless chap like me," he said. "I'd like to take those ferns and tie them round his trunk, and. . . ."

He stopped speaking and his eyes widened. If he could tie something together with those old dry ferns. . . . He could take those broken branches. . . . With a cry he jumped up and started to work.

Herman, meanwhile, had retired to doze nearby and to watch the pit. After all, he wanted no harm to come to Grump. Life would be so boring without the little caveman to liven things up. He watched with interest, and eventually he was rewarded.

Two branches slowly poked up from the pit. They jogged and wavered for a moment, then rested against the side of the hole. Soon afterwards there was a grunting noise and Grump's face appeared above the ground. He looked about him like a suspicious rabbit, but he didn't see Herman. Finally, he climbed out and turned to haul the branches up after him. They were joined side by side with ropes of twisted fern. Grump looked at them proudly.

"What a smart caveman I am," he said. "Takes a brain to make something like this. Now what shall I call it? What about – yes, what about calling it a ladder?"

Grump had reason to be pleased. With his ladder he could do all sorts of things: climb tall trees, get eggs from the topmost ledges, find a new cave so high up that no animal could reach him.

"I can even hide from that great furry faggot, Herman," Grump smirked. "Not that I'm scared of him. If he were here now I'd tie a knot in his trunk."

Grump shouldn't have said that. As he did so, Herman blew a bellow that set Grump's ears ringing. He didn't stop to hear another one. He seized his ladder and ran away so quickly that his legs seemed to vanish in a haze.

Mammoths don't often laugh, yet anyone watching Herman would have said that's just what he was doing. His mighty shoulders shook, and his trunk swung like a pendulum from side to side. He watched Grump until he was out of sight. Then, with a last toot of his trunk, Herman settled down once more to doze in the sunshine.

2

Grump in the Swim

"Why do they always pick on me?"

Grump was muttering to himself as he sagged over his fishing line by the icy lake. He peered down at the reflection of his face in the water. It looked even gloomier than usual.

The other Ice Age men had driven him from the best fishing spot by the lake and he hadn't caught anything all morning. What was worse, he could hear a dreadful buzzing noise, which never stopped. Buzz, buzz, buzz! It came from behind him, where the trees edged close to the lake.

Grump turned around, and suddenly he felt worse than ever.

"It's him! It's him again, as if I didn't have enough troubles already!"

It was Herman the mammoth, strolling happily in the morning sunshine. He was humming untunefully to himself, but that wasn't the noise that was plaguing Grump. Instead, the buzzing seemed to come from a small black cloud which hovered by Herman's head.

Grump frowned and peered more closely.

"It's a trick, that's what it is," he muttered. "That moth-eaten monster wants to make a fool of me again."

Any other time Grump might have made himself ignore the mammoth. He'd got the worst of encounters with Herman before. But this was just too much! He reached for a rock near his feet.

"Take that, you cowardly carpet-bag!" He hurled the rock with all his might at the mammoth's head.

It bounced as harmlessly as a balloon off Herman's hard skull. He turned a mild reproachful eye on Grump.

"Go away! Go away and polish your tusks or I'll throw another rock at you!"

Grump was on his feet now, shouting and waving, rather scared at what he had done. To his amazement, Herman whisked his trunk once or twice, then trundled off into the trees.

"Huh, that taught him!" And, satisfied, Grump returned to his fishing. Then something hit him on the back of the neck – a large sticky object that almost sent him tumbling into the lake.

"Help, I'm being bombarded!" Grump scrambled like a mad spider to behind a boulder. Finally, he peered nervously over the top, just in time to see Herman strolling back into the trees.

"What a dirty trick, hitting me when my back was turned. Cheat! Come back and I'll tie a knot in your trunk!"

Brave, now that Herman was leaving, Grump was on his feet again, yelling and waving the sticky yellow object that the mammoth had thrown at him. At last he sat down and looked at his hands. They were covered with yellow goo.

He licked his fingers cautiously. His eyes widened. He licked them again, eagerly this time. He had never in his life tasted anything so sweet, so toothsome. Soon he was sucking the sticky yellow object excitedly.

"Mmm, it's delicious! Mmm, it's marvellous!" he exclaimed. "Far too good for a tatty old mammoth. I've got to find out where he gets it."

So, wherever he went all the next day, Herman had Grump close behind, slipping from rock to rock and tree to tree.

"Stupid thing couldn't see a dancing dinosaur!" muttered Grump as he crept along. "As soon as he finds some more of that lovely yellow stuff, I'll have it."

But Grump was becoming rather tired of following Herman. The mammoth roamed far and wide, using the thorniest, dampest paths, and always he had that wretched buzzing cloud with him. Buzz, buzz, buzz! It was driving Grump crazy. Only the thought of that delicious sticky stuff kept him going.

"What's he up to now?" Grump stopped suspiciously as Herman paused beneath a tree.

Suddenly the noise from the small cloud dancing around Herman's head became frantic. Herman reached with his trunk into the crook of the tree and groped around. Soon yellow liquid was trickling down the outside of his trunk.

"That's it! That's where he keeps the stuff!"

In triumph, Grump darted forward. For once, in his eagerness, he forgot his fear of the great beast. He seized a long stick and drove the mammoth away.

"Serves him right for trying to hog it," Grump muttered as he scrambled up the tree. "Besides, I'm doing him a favour. It only makes his fur all sticky."

As he spoke, Grump found a large hollow in the tree, rimmed with sticky yellow. He thrust his hand inside. It was then that he learnt the meaning of Herman's hovering, buzzing cloud.

"Ooooh! Ow! Eee!"

With a yell of pain, Grump leaped from the tree. Now he had a cloud of his own round his head; a cloud of huge, angry bees, determined to punish this intruder. Unlike Herman, poor Grump had no thick fur to save him from their stings. He danced, he slapped, he shouted, but it was no use.

"Oooh! Stop it at once! Ouch!"

Suddenly Grump was heaved up by the back of his rabbit-skin coat. He was carried like a wriggling sack through the forest. The bees were still stinging him, but he was too scared to notice that now. The thing that was holding him was long and grey, and looked very much like a mammoth's trunk. Herman had captured him!

"Put me down! Please put me down, and you can have your rotten old yellow stuff," Grump pleaded.

He was still shouting when they reached the lake. Herman looked around anxiously. He knew how ill Grump would be if the bees carried on stinging much longer. Yes, Grump deserved all that he was getting, but Herman had a kind heart. He must put Grump somewhere safe from the bees. Herman lumbered to the lakeside.

"No, not in there! Please, don't...." Even as he yelled, Grump's mouth was filled with water as the mammoth plunged him into the lake.

"Help, save me, someone!" Grump splut-

tered as Herman whisked him up for air. "He's trying to drown me. Help!"

Down he went again, arms and legs flailing. Up down, up down, like a bunch of wet rags. It was on the fifth time that Grump gave a desperate twist, tore free from Herman's grasp, and threshed away.

Some moments passed before he realized that he was still afloat.

"Hey, look at me, I'm staying on top," he shouted. "I'm not going under like I usually do!"

He gazed about him in wonder as his splashing arms and legs carried him away from the shore where Herman stood.

"Fooled you, didn't I?" he yelled back at the mammoth in triumph. "I'm – what shall I call it? – yes, I'm swimming!"

Grump was afraid of the water no longer. He didn't even mind its coldness. He was filled with the joy of floating, of surging forward. Soon he was even brave enough to duck his head down to look at the fish gliding in their own grey world.

Fish! Suddenly Grump thought how amazed and scared the other Ice Age men would be to see him swimming. Scared enough to run away and leave their catch of fish on the lake shore.

"Fish for supper tonight," he chuckled to himself. "Lots of lovely fish!" He turned and began to swim across the lake to where the other men were fishing.

And Herman, who stood watching him on the shore, heard a sound, a very unusual sound. It was Grump laughing.

The mammoth stood there for a while after the little man was out of sight. Then, lifting his trunk as if in farewell, he turned and walked into the forest.

3

Grump the Artist

"I've got it! I've got it at last!"

Grump's eyes sparkled with excitement as he crouched in the centre of his cave. They reflected the light of something that danced and flickered before him. It was a gaily burning fire. Grump had never been so pleased with himself.

"Said I couldn't do it, didn't they? Laughed at me, they did."

Grump hadn't lit the fire himself. At that time no caveman could make fire. But it had been a dry summer. Lightning had struck a tree in the forest, and set it alight. Only Grump of all the cavemen had thought of taking a smouldering stick from the fire. The others had mocked him, but now he had a small fire of his very own.

"And it's lovely, simply lovely!" he chortled. "Won't they be jealous when the cold weather comes."

The catch was that the weather was still warm and Grump's cave was so full of smoke that he could hardly breathe. At last he could stand it no more.

"I'll just pop outside for some fresh air. Need more wood for my marvellous fire, anyway."

He strode outside. Not a caveman was in sight. They were all resting in damp caves, or fishing by the lake. Grump chuckled.

"I think I'll stroll down to the lake and tell them about my new invention," he said, "just to make them envious."

Grump felt unusually contented as he walked towards the shore, gathering wood as he went. He imagined a wonderful cosy winter, with a fire glowing in his cave. He might even let the other cave people warm themselves by it – if they stopped laughing at him.

"After all," he told himself, "I'm a pretty

clever caveman. Well, perhaps not pretty. . . ."

Suddenly he stopped talking and walking. He had arrived at the lakeside, and an interesting sight greeted him. Herman was in the water, cooling himself. Only his trunk stuck out above the surface. But Grump could see his hairy coat fluffed up in the water, so that he looked like a huge mop. Grump laughed.

"I even feel friendly to that hairy big balloon today," he said. "The poor old chap is so hot. I wonder if I can help?"

Such thoughts were strange ones for Grump, but now he tramped to a nearby glacier and broke off the largest lump of ice he could manage. By the time he had dragged it back to the lake he was quite exhausted. He wiped his brow and gazed at the water. Herman was still there, his eyes closed.

"I'll give him a surprise," Grump said.

"Won't he be pleased when I make him nice and cool!"

He waded into the lake. Then, pushing the ice in front of him on top of the water, he swam towards Herman. The mammoth did not stir. He was much too happy enjoying the coolness of the water to notice Grump. It was a pity that he opened his mouth to yawn just as the caveman swam up to him.

Grump was startled. The ice suddenly disappeared from sight into the cavern of Herman's mouth. Herman was startled too, very startled. All at once he seemed to be swallowing the largest ice-cream ever. It was a horrible feeling. He opened his eyes to find himself looking at Grump.

"No," Grump stuttered, "you don't understand. I was only trying to help. It wasn't a trick, honestly!"

He didn't stop to explain. A gleam in Herman's eye told him it would be dangerous to do so. In a flash he was swimming for shore. Herman was close behind him, and far from friendly.

It was lucky for Grump that Herman had been in the lake. Only his water-sodden fur stopped him catching the caveman in the first few steps. As it was, the mammoth had to stop and shake himself like a giant dog. Soon the forest around him was as wet as if there had been a thunderstorm.

Even so, Grump only just beat Herman to the safety of his cave. He dodged inside, and bolted into a crack in the wall where the mammoth could not reach him. Herman didn't bother. He had already decided how he would punish the caveman for what seemed a mean trick.

He waited, his cheeks bulging with water and his trunk stiff as a hose. The moment Grump peered from his hiding place, Herman blew with all his might. A stream of water almost knocked Grump over. He clung to the rock, his teeth chattering, until the dousing was finished. Then he looked out cautiously again. Herman was lumbering away from the cave.

"Humph! That's the last time I do you a good turn!" Grump complained.

Grump shook a damp fist at Herman. The mammoth stopped and looked back. He had quite enjoyed the chase, and he could never bear a grudge for long. He waved his trunk and continued towards the lake. He needed to cool down again.

As for Grump, he was far from happy. When he turned back into his cave, an awful sight met his eyes. His gaily burning fire was gone. In its place were a few soggy sticks. Herman's hose had worked too well!

"My fire! He's ruined my lovely fire!" wailed Grump, and fell on his knees by the

damp cinders. "I'll never forgive him for this!"

He blew, he coaxed, but it was useless. His marvellous fire was dead for ever.

"And I'll never get another one, unless there's a forest fire again. Oh, what I could do to that mammoth!"

He threw the charred sticks away from him. One scraped down the smooth wall as it fell, and left a most interesting mark. Grump frowned and moved close. "Funny, it's a long curly mark. It looks like Herman's trunk. How did that happen?"

c

He picked up the stick and ran the burnt end down the wall. Another black line appeared. He tried again. One more line came, and together they looked even more like a mammoth's trunk. Grump was suddenly trembling with excitement.

"What a wonderful invention!" he cried. "Better than a smelly old fire any day. This way I can make pictures of anything I want!"

It was evening when Herman returned to Grump's cave. He felt guilty about the little man. Perhaps he had been rather unkind to him. He stopped in the cave doorway, and his eyes widened in amazement. Every smooth spot in Grump's home was covered in drawings, big drawings, of every sort of animal imaginable. And Grump was still drawing busily.

Herman looked closely. Grump seemed to be drawing a very strange creature. It was big, it was shaggy, and it had two tusks on either side of a long, long trunk. Herman shook his head. He'd never seen an animal like that before. How strange of Grump to think of such a thing!

Herman curled his trunk and rubbed his tusks thoughtfully. Then he turned and sauntered towards the lake once more, for a last wallow before night came.

4

Grump on the Boil

"If I don't find something to eat soon I – I'll chew my jacket!"

Grump groaned and looked down at the rabbit-skin jacket he always wore. It was a very thin and sad-looking jacket, but Grump was thin and sad himself that morning. All he had eaten for breakfast was a few stringy roots. There was nothing else left near his cave.

"Horrid stuff! Not enough to keep a dodo alive," he sighed. "What I need is a good square meal."

Grump had wandered a long way in search of food. Now he was in a strange part of the country. Hot springs welled up through the ground. Lakes of warm mud spluttered in the sunlight. There were even some trees with round red berries on them. Grump's eyes brightened.

"Fine! Those will make a good meal."

He climbed a tree and stuffed a handful of the berries into his mouth. Then spat them out. They were very bitter.

"Nasty things," Grump grumbled. "No right to be here unless they're some use."

He was about to climb down from the tree when he saw something interesting. At the end of a branch was a large nest. In it lay four eggs.

"Food!" Grump cried. "Fresh eggs are just what I need."

He scrambled eagerly up to the nest and perched there, looking at his prize. They were large eggs, big enough even for Grump's appetite. He broke one carefully and ate it. He grimaced. It was raw and horrible, but since nobody had yet learnt how to cook, Grump's food often tasted nasty.

"Oh, well, it's the best I can get," he said.

Stuffing the remaining eggs inside his jacket,
he turned to climb down the tree. Once more
something caught his eye. It was far below
him, in a lake of mud.

"I do believe – it can't be – it is! What's that
crazy mammoth up to now?"

In the middle of the mud-lake was a large
brown lump, and from it came a sound of
humming. It was Herman, having a mud-
bath. His fur was patched with mud, and at
intervals his trunk flipped a splodgy lump on

top of his head. He was very happy.

"Great loon," Grump said, "whatever does he think he's doing?"

He sat in the tree, fascinated, while Herman rolled in the mud. At last the mammoth stood up, and strolled over to where a cold waterfall was tumbling down from a cliff. He rinsed himself. Then, with a shake of his head and a sharp trumpeting, he returned to his mud-bath.

Grump's eyes gleamed. His hunger was forgotten. It wasn't often that he had a chance like this. He quickly clambered from the tree and scampered up a hill. Soon he was at the spot where Herman's waterfall splashed over the cliff. He looked at it thoughtfully.

"Not enough water to wash a starved mouse. What that mammoth needs is a nice lot of water, all at once."

He started to pull a fallen log across the narrow gap in the cliff through which the water fell.

Herman, meanwhile, lay contentedly in the mud, blowing the occasional bubble. Finally, he rose with a sigh and trudged to his waterfall for a last rinse. But the waterfall had vanished! Not a drop of water was tumbling from the cliff. Herman stared upwards in amazement.

That was the moment Grump had been waiting for. It was his signal to pull away the log. A great pool of water had been trapped behind it. Now it surged over the cliff with a roar and sploshed down on Herman. The mammoth was helpless. Large as he was, he was swept back to the mud-lake. He lay there breathless, blowing great spurts of water through his trunk. Grump was delighted.

"That'll teach him," he said, and strolled down the hill. He paused by the muddy pool in which Herman lay.

"What are you doing there, hollow head?" he cried. "Fancy playing in the mud at your age!"

That was more than Herman could bear. He reared up with a bellow that set the hills rumbling. And Grump found a muddy mountain thundering towards him. He turned and ran as fast as his short legs would carry him.

But unfortunately for Grump, there was nowhere to go. The trees were too short to hide in, and there were no caves handy. There were only lakes of bubbling mud or steaming water. Herman's trunk touched Grump's shoulder.

"Oh, no you don't!" Grump shouted. "You don't catch me!"

With a mighty bound, he leaped into the nearest pool. Luckily, it was hot but not boiling. Luckily, too, Herman couldn't swim. Grump was soon splashing about in the middle of the lake while Herman stood in the shallows.

"Missed me again!" Grump shouted in triumph. "Planned to give me a mud-bath, didn't you?"

To tell the truth, Herman didn't know what he had intended to do with the little caveman. In any case, his normal good nature had now returned. It hardly seemed worth chasing Grump. The mammoth settled down contentedly in the hot water.

That was all very well for Herman with his fur and thick skin. For Grump it was different.

The water really felt extremely warm after a time. His head was singing, and he felt more and more like a boiled potato. But he dare not leave the lake while Herman was nearby.

Herman had a delightful bathe that day. He was in no rush. He'd quite forgotten about Grump when he finally left the lake and strolled away. Even then Grump did not emerge for some time. At last he plucked up courage, and splattered ashore.

"Great bully," Grump complained to himself, "keeping me in the water all that time. I've never been so clean. It's horrible!"

He reached inside his jacket and pulled out one of the eggs.

"And now it's too late for hunting, and all I've got are these horrid eggs. Ugh, I can't bear them!"

He hurled the egg in disgust at a rock. It bounced. Grump stopped in surprise.

"Funny, it should have broken. What's wrong?"

He bent to pick up the egg. It was hot, and where part of the shell had cracked away, he could see something white inside. Grump put a piece in his mouth. It was delicious, smooth, firm and tasty. And inside was a well-cooked yoke. Grump couldn't believe his luck.

"How did it happen? How did they change?"

He looked round at the steaming lake.

"Being in there must have done something to them. It – it *cooked* them. I need never eat raw eggs again!"

Grump stood watching the warm lake for a few moments in wonder. Then he started back

towards his cave. He bit into the eggs as he walked and sang to himself between mouthfuls. Life wasn't so bad after all.

5

Grump Strikes Back

"Crazy lot!"

Grump snorted as he peered from the edge of the forest.

"Crazy lot, what *do* they think they look like?"

Strange sounds floated through the air. In the clearing before him the other cavemen were having their monthly dance. Not that it could be called a dance. For one thing, there was no music. Instead, the men shuffled round in a large circle, moaning mournfully. Each wore a strange hat made from birds' feathers. They looked very odd.

"Huh, fancy thinking I'd join them. I'm not so stupid."

But Grump was not telling the truth. He, too, had made himself a hat. And he had turned up to dance in it. But the usual thing had happened. The other men had driven him away.

Grump's nose wrinkled at the memory.

"Well, they can keep their dance," he muttered. "I'm off for a walk."

He set off into the forest, the feathers nodding dolefully on his head. Poor Grump badly wanted to be friends with the other men. Yet here he was, walking alone through the silent night.

Silent? He had walked far from the dance by now, but he still seemed to hear the cavemen's awful moaning ahead of him. He frowned.

"Must have walked in a big circle. Except – yes – I've heard that voice before!"

He grunted with excitement and crept forward. Soon he was on the edge of another clearing, and his eyes widened.

"It's him! It's that crazy mammoth again! What's he up to now?"

In the clearing, under the trailing creepers which hung down from the trees, was Herman. He was circling round, shuffling his feet carefully one before the other and humming like a mad bee. Grump watched for a while, then suddenly giggled.

"He's dancing!" Grump exclaimed. "He's seen us dancing, and he's copying. Of all the barmy beasts!"

Grump watched again. It was like seeing a hairy house doing a jig. Then the caveman slid quietly back among the trees with a mischievous grin.

At any other time Herman would have been alert, but tonight he was concentrating on his dancing.

The first thing he knew was when a creeper dropped down in a loop around his feet. He looked up. Grump was grinning at him from a tree above, and already lowering another creeper around Herman's legs.

"Got you!" Grump shouted in triumph.

It was hopeless for Herman to trumpet and struggle. In a trice Grump had the creepers tight and was pulling with all his might. Herman tottered, and finally fell with a crash.

"Now I've caught you, floppy ears," Grump cried, and jumped down beside the fallen mammoth.

But strangely enough, Herman didn't seem one bit put out. His eyes gleamed with laughter. Grump gazed at him suspiciously. For a rough-haired animal, Herman could be awfully slippery. Perhaps he'd better check that those creepers were tight.

It's quite true that Herman was not worried. He lay there placidly, wondering what the caveman would do next. The feathers on Grump's hat changed that. As he bent down they whisked the mammoth just under the trunk. Herman had never been tickled before and he hated it. He squealed and struggled to get up.

"Threaten me, would you, bonehead?" said Grump, who had leaped three yards away in alarm.

D

Herman sneezed, and the whole forest shook. Grump reached up and touched his feather hat in understanding.

"So that's it," he grinned. "You don't like your nose tickled? Hate to have some more of it, I suppose?"

In a flash he was beside Herman and tickling him for all he was worth. Herman was helpless with mammoth laughter as the tickling went on and on; then he could bear it no longer. With a roar he heaved to his feet and snapped the creepers round his legs.

Grump took to his heels with a squeal.

The chase was a nightmare: plunging through forests, dodging dinosaurs, leaping snakes. And Herman was always at his heels.

"Can't go on!" Grump spluttered. "Must hide or he'll catch me and send me four ways at once."

Just in time, Grump saw a hollow log on the forest floor. He dived inside and scrambled out of Herman's reach. He lay there, panting, as the mammoth paced to and fro outside.

"Haha, old tin tusks, I've done it again. I've outwitted you, dumbchops!"

By now Grump was highly pleased with himself. Herman would never winkle him out of this hiding place.

Bonk!

Grump's ears rang. Bonk! Bonk! Bonk! Herman was hitting the log with a stick, and each time it shook and echoed with a great booming noise.

"Stop it! Stop it before my ears fall off!" Grump pleaded.

It was no use. Herman thumped the fallen log until the forest rang with its booming. He didn't stop until he felt the little man had been punished enough. He gave the log one last bonk that set it ringing, then strolled off into the forest. He had had a most enjoyable evening.

Five minutes passed before the dazed Grump dared to crawl out.

"That mammoth never fights fair," he complained. "Fancy trying to boom a man to death!"

He picked up a stick and gloomily whacked

the log. Bonk! It was rather a pleasant sound if you weren't actually inside. He hit it again. Bonk! Soon the forest and far beyond were throbbing with a strange new sound as Grump tried different kinds of beats. He was so happy doing it, he didn't notice the other cavemen arrive.

"What do you call that thing?" one of them asked.

"Eh? Leave me alone!" Grump cried, thinking that Herman had returned.

"What do you call it?" the man insisted.

Grump thought very hard.

"Well, it's – um – it's called a drum. Very magical. Only I can work it."

He banged the log several times, and the feet of the cavemen shuffled restlessly. Grump saw his chance, and smiled loftily.

"I'll bonk it for you to dance to, if you want. You'll have to ask me nicely, though," he said.

The cavemen looked at each other, then surged forward noisily. The hollow log and Grump were carried shoulder high back to his cave.

From then on, Grump was the star of the show. He sat proudly at the centre of it all, playing his hardest, quite convinced that it was he who had invented drumming.

Only Herman, who watched from the trees, his trunk waving gently to the drumbeat, knew any better.

6

Grump's Cold Feet

"Wheeeeeee! Wheeeeeee!"

Grump's eyes were wide, but his mouth was even wider as he gazed upwards.

"Wheeeeeee! Wheeeeeee!" he shrilled.

High above him a giant bird circled slowly in the sunlight. Grump watched enviously. Then his eyes dropped from the bird to his own feet, standing in the snow. They were blue with cold. He sighed. How lovely it must be to fly! No tramping through the snow. No feeling your bare toes go numb with cold. Grump shivered. With a last glance up at the bird, he turned downhill.

As he trudged down the mountainside his face crinkled. He was thinking. Flying should be quite easy, he told himself. It was just a matter of running quickly, flapping your arms hard enough. In no time you'd be high in the sky, with the horrid snow far below.

He started to run, flapping his arms as he went. As he did so he whistled again: "Wheeeeeee! Wheeeeeee!"

It was no use. Hard as he flapped and quickly as his stubby legs ran, he did not take off. Not until he tripped over a bump, that is. Then he took off most satisfactorily, only to land again on his nose four yards onwards.

He sat up grumbling. Was that an amused gurgle he heard coming from somewhere near by? He looked around sharply. A great, good-natured face was just disappearing behind a rock. Herman, of course! Grump grunted. He climbed to his feet and continued downhill with all the dignity he could manage.

Herman shook his head. He had been worried about Grump lately. He was quite used to the little caveman grumbling to himself, but this business of dashing along and waving his arms was strange. Herman decided to keep an eye on Grump, and settled back to rest in the snow.

Grump, meanwhile, had arrived back at his chilly cave and sat down bad-temperedly.

"Cheeky big lollipop, laughing at me like that," he growled. "Thinks I can't fly, does he? Well, I'll show him!"

But why couldn't he fly? Was he all that different from a bird? Grump looked down at himself. His legs and body were much like a bird's, and his funny face wasn't much different either. He looked at his arms, and gave a crow of joy.

"Of course, I need stuff to cover my arms," he yelled. "I need wings! What can I use?"

In a flash he was searching through the rubbish at the back of his cave. There were many things there. A bent stick for scratching his back, a round stone for bouncing off the walls when he was bored, a peacock's feather for tiggling his toes. At last he gave a cry.

"Here they are! They'll do beautifully!"

He danced around, waving two rabbit

skins. They were old, tatty skins, too small to use for making a jacket.

"These are my wings," he cried. "With these on my arms I'll fly so high that my toes will never be cold again."

Still shouting with delight, he bolted from his cave and up the mountainside. He was a long way up before he began to wonder how to attach the skins to his arms. He paused to think.

"If I wrap them round tightly they won't flap like a bird's wings. I'll probably fall and bonk my nose again. I need something to hang them on my arms just right."

His eyes searched the bleak, snowy mountain. There was nothing suitable for tying on the rabbit skins. Then he saw something behind a rock, and his eyes widened with glee.

"That's just the stuff I need," he giggled. "If only I can get a handful."

He crept furtively towards the rock. Resting by it was a mighty grey mound, covered in warm, shaggy hair. It was Herman, sleeping. Grump reached forward nervously.

"Got it!" he cried. A moment later he was scuttling up the hillside with a handful of Herman's wiry hair.

Poor Herman! One moment he was sleeping peacefully, and the next he looked up to see Grump capering above him.

"Thought I couldn't do it, didn't you, clever boots?" Grump was calling. "Well, now you're going to see me fly!"

Hurriedly Grump made holes in the rabbit skins, and threaded the hair through them. Then he tied the skins to his arms. He flapped. It seemed to work. He was sure he'd almost lifted from the ground. He flapped again. Yes, he was certain of it.

Herman by now had heaved to his feet and was watching with interest. Why was Grump shouting so? And why was he running and shaking his arms? Suddenly Herman's interest changed to alarm. Grump had turned and was running faster and faster. He was heading directly for a spot where the mountain disappeared in a sheer drop. He was going to jump over! Herman lumbered forward.

"I'm off!" Grump shouted, as he came to the cliff's edge. And off he was, with a great leap. He flapped his arms like a bird, and closed his eyes to enjoy the feeling of flying. Yet it was odd. It was not at all as he'd imagined it. In fact, he didn't seem to be flying at all.

He wasn't! He opened his eyes and found himself swaying in mid-air exactly where he'd leaped over the cliff. He twisted his head to look over his shoulder. Above him Herman's face looked down anxiously, and a long trunk stretched down firmly gripping Grump's jacket.

Grump struggled and gave a shout of alarm.

"Let me go, you interfering busybody! Let me fly, will you?"

But Herman had no intention of letting Grump fly. He had only caught the caveman in the nick of time as he dived from the cliff. If Grump had fallen. . . . Herman shuddered at the thought. He turned downhill and carried Grump towards safer ground.

Grump remembered the large handful of

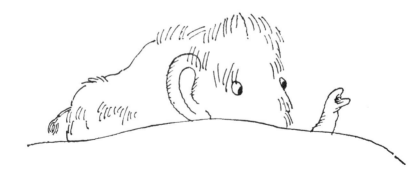

hair he had pulled from Herman, and his knees went weak. What did the mammoth mean to do to him? He struggled more desperately than ever.

"Be careful with me! All this fuss over a few hairs when you've got so many. Put me down, you big bully!"

With those words Grump twisted free. He fell to the snow and skidded down the mountainside before Herman could stop him. It was a nice sensation really, and when he hit a bump and soared into the air, Grump squawked with delight. The hillside dipped sharply away below him. He was flying!

But again it didn't feel right. It felt more like falling. However hard he flapped his arms, he dropped down and down towards the snow.

Thump! Luckily for Grump the fall was not far, and a snowdrift was waiting to catch him when he landed head-first. His legs waved for a moment like socks on a washing line, then he pulled himself free. He sat up angrily.

"Rotten things, they're no use at all!" he growled, pulling the rabbit skins from his arms and flinging them down.

He stared at them gloomily, and then at his feet, curling in the freezing snow.

"Now I'll have to walk home instead, and my poor feet will get colder than ever."

He kicked grumpily at the rabbit skin, and its warm fur tingled his frozen toes. He frowned and bent forward.

"Nice feeling," he said. "I wonder if somehow I could fix those skins to my feet?"

He knelt down busily for a few moments, and then stood up. On each foot he had a rabbit skin, fur inwards, and Herman's hair tied them on tightly. Grump wriggled a toe. He could feel it getting warm already. A wonderful glow was spreading through him.

It was lovely. It was something he'd never known before – warm feet!

"Huh, this beats flying any day," he told himself. "Who wants to whizz round like a silly old bird when you can walk with warm feet?"

And Grump could not only walk. He could run if he wanted to. He could dance through the snow, and never a freezing drop would chill his feet. And dance he did, whirling round and round in joy down the mountain-side. Far above him, Herman watched with a puzzled face until the spinning, crazy figure had disappeared from sight in the misty mountain air.

7

Grump on the Slide

Bop! Something cold hit Grump on his nose as he stepped from his cave. Bop! Bop! Bop! More objects hit him, icy objects like freezing suet puddings. Grump didn't hesitate. He ran. He'd met those things before.

"Funny old Grump! Silly old Grump! Come and play snowballs with us!" cried a voice.

"Not him, he's scared," yelled another voice. "My Dad says he's the most cowardly caveman ever."

Grump scowled. In the clearing by his cave a group of children were playing snowballs. He had been just the target they wanted. They grinned at him.

"Coo, look at him frown!" one of them said. "Bet his face would make the mountain melt."

Grump growled. He didn't blame the children. If their parents were always laughing at him, how could he expect the youngsters to be different? With a sigh, he turned away.

"Cheeky icicles! Frozen faggots!" he muttered to himself as he walked up the snowy mountainside.

Of course he was upset. And it was only natural to want to take it out on someone else – like a cheery mammoth, for instance. Grump's eyes widened as he heard something ahead of him.

"Mmyaww . . . mmyaww . . . mmyaww . . . ."

It was Herman, humming to himself, sitting in the soft snow. He loved its coolness against his furry body. Where it touched him it melted, and turned into steam. So he sat there, his trunk raised, looking like a great steaming kettle.

"Got him at last!" Grump chuckled to himself. "I've got that fat furry thing just where I want him!"

He circled out of sight of the happy mammoth. Ten minutes later he was above him on the mountainside. He peered out from behind a tall, flat rock, rubbing his hands in glee.

"What I need to start with is a nice lot of snowballs, big ones for bouncing off mammoths' heads."

Soon his short fingers were moulding snowballs. A pile beside him grew quickly. He peered out again. Herman was still sitting peacefully below.

"Right, you hairy house, this is where you get what for!"

The first that Herman knew of Grump's attack was when snowballs started to shower down on him. He lifted his head inquiringly, and then shook himself mildly as one hit him in the eye. It was all very puzzling – puzzling, that is, until he glimpsed Grump's gleeful face. The little man was at it again. So he wanted to play?

Herman rose patiently to his feet, and the mountain seemed to shake as he lumbered behind a tree. Grump smirked.

"Thinks I can't see him, does he?" Grump said. "I'll show him!"

The pile of snowballs beside him was almost gone. He bent down hurriedly to make some more. When the last one was shaped to his satisfaction, he chuckled.

"Right, this is where I finish him off!"

He jumped up with a cry of triumph from behind the flat rock, his mouth open wide. It was a pity he did that. A snowball from Herman plopped right in. It was like having a mouth full of freezing needles. And more were coming. Snowballs flew from Herman's trunk like bullets from a gun.

67

"Ooo! Ow! Stop it!" Grump cried, holding to the rock for support. Snowballs battered him everywhere and slid coldly down his neck. But that wasn't all. The flat rock to which he clung slowly toppled over. At last it lay on the snow, with Grump on top of it, eyes closed. He opened them to find himself moving.

Herman was most surprised when he looked up from making more snowballs. Grump was sliding by him, slowly at first, then faster and faster as the hillside became steeper. Herman shook his head in wonder. What was the little man up to now?

Grump wasn't up to anything. He was clinging to the rock with all his might as it zoomed down the slope. He had never travelled so quickly. Trees, rocks and rivers flashed by him. Startled animals leaped aside as he whizzed by them. And all the time Grump held on, praying that he would not fall. Somehow he steered the slab of rock down the mountainside until the slope became gentle and the snow even. In fact, he even began to enjoy himself.

68

"Mmm, not a bad way to travel," he said. "Quick, easy and good for escaping from crazy mammoths."

In the distance he could see the children still snowballing near his cave. He steered the rock towards them. They jumped aside in amazement when he slid placidly through them and stopped not far away. They ran forward.

"What's that, Grump?" they asked eagerly, crowding around him. "How did you do it?"

Grump waved airily at the rock on which he had made his perilous journey.

"It's something I've just invented," he said. "I call it – I call it a sledge!"

He looked at the children. For the first time in his life they were not laughing at him. They were actually staring at him in admiration! He smiled.

"If you want, I'll show you how it's done," he offered. "It's clever but simple, like all my ideas."

"Please, Grump! Oh please!" they cried, and clung to his arms as if he were the most important man in the world.

Grump straightened proudly. "Come on,
then, follow me. But mind you behave your-
selves!"

Not long afterwards, high on the mountain,
Herman was surprised to see Grump and a
happy band of children coming towards him.
He slipped behind a tree, eager for another
game of snowballs. But they took no notice of
him. Instead, with Grump's help, they each
chose a flat rock and placed it on the snow.

Soon they were all whizzing downwards with Grump in the lead, shouting with delight.

Herman watched them a little sadly. Just when he had learned to throw snowballs like a human they were off doing something else. Something that even the cleverest mammoth couldn't manage.

He shook his head slowly, settled down in the snow once more, and sat there steaming gently in the sun.

8

Grump's Party

"Hmm, let's see. Three boiled eggs each, a honeycomb, some blackberries and some fruit juice. That should do nicely."

Grump stepped back to look at the large flat rock that was his table. Today he was having his very first party, and he wanted everything to look perfect. He had even decorated his cave with creepers and flowers to make it more cheerful. He went to the doorway of his cave and looked out anxiously.

"They should be here soon now. Hope they're not late."

His guests were to be the children whom he had taught to sledge. He looked across the rocky ground towards their caves. All was quiet. He shook his head.

"They promised to come. They were quite excited, specially when I promised to play my drum. Surely they wouldn't miss that?"

He turned back into his cave, planning party games for after the food. Hunt the Turtle, perhaps? Hide and Seek? Musical Stones? His eyes brightened. It was nice having the children for friends. It made all the difference having people to talk to.

"My drum! Must have my drum," Grump muttered.

He hurried to the high ledge where he kept the hollow log that he used as a drum. He could only just reach it, and as he did so his foot slipped. Down he crashed with the log on top of him.

Booooing! The noise almost burst Grump's ears. He climbed to his feet, grumbling, and set the drum upright.

"Silly thing! Wish it wouldn't make that noise. It sounded like thunder."

It was thunder! Grump turned in dismay towards his doorway. Outside, rain was falling like a million glass splinters. The sky was black and thunder was cracking. He ran to look out. The ground between him and the other caves had vanished. In its place was a foaming river where the downpour ran away. Grump gazed in despair.

"It can't be – not today of all days! My party will be ruined. Nobody will even get here."

Still he stared, trying to tell himself that the children would come. At last he turned back into his cave with a sigh.

"It's no use, they'll never make it. They probably didn't intend to come anyway," he added bitterly.

He glanced at the gay food laid out on his table, and sat down sulkily in the dimmest corner of his cave. The rain crashed down outside. It was half an hour before he moved again. He looked up. Something big and very damp was moving in his doorway. He pressed back into his corner.

"Something's coming in," he whispered. "What is it?"

A loud sneeze gave him the answer.

"It's that pesky mammoth! What are you doing in here, wool ears? Go away! Shoo!"

Herman gazed at Grump mildly but did not move. For one thing, it was still raining very hard, and Herman hated rain. It made his hair soggy. That was why he had taken refuge in a cave. Now that he had found it was Grump's cave, he was much too interested to go.

He looked round him. The small caveman had made so many changes. Who would have expected him to decorate it with flowers and creepers? It was quite comfy. And what were those things on the stone table? He licked the honeycombs. Delicious! He munched a blackberry or two. Delightful! When he reached for a boiled egg, Grump could stand it no more.

"Leave those things alone!" he shouted. "They're for my friends. Stop trunking them around!"

Herman was so startled by Grump's angry cry that he let go of the egg. It flew from his trunk across the cave. Grump caught it just before it hit the floor. Herman regarded him with pleasure and tossed another one. Grump caught that, too.

"Mind what you're doing, you'll smash the things," Grump cried out, but it was already too late. Herman was tossing another and another. Soon eggs were flying like snowballs, and Grump was darting to catch them. Not that he left it at that. He found himself tossing them back, and Herman just as easily caught them. All at once it was a game, a very tiring game. After ten minutes of it they were both exhausted. Grump reached for a drink.

"No you don't, hairy egg thrower," he said, as Herman looked at the drink hopefully. "Fruit juice isn't for mammoths."

He drank, but all the time he felt Herman's eyes on him. At last it was too much to bear. He turned.

"If you want a drink, you'll find one there," he said. "The rain drips through the roof into a hollow."

He gestured towards one side of the cave. Herman went obediently to drink there. Grump watched him, and frowned in thought.

"Crazy animal. Who'd have thought he'd enjoy playing catch? Wonder if he likes drums, too?"

Grump reached for his drum. He looked at Herman and thumped it. The mammoth's feet moved. He banged the drum once more, and Herman's huge feet shuffled in time. Grump laughed.

"Come on then, beetle boots," he ordered, "don't just stand there. Dance!"

And dance Herman did. His feet pounded up and down, his great head nodded, as Grump played louder and louder. Bonketty bonk! Round and round Herman lumbered, faster and faster, until he was quite dizzy. Bonketty bonk bonk!

Suddenly Grump found that he was enjoying himself. Suddenly he was glad that the downpour had brought Herman to his cave. Herman was glad, too. He closed his eyes in enjoyment. That was a mistake. His whirling trunk hit Grump behind the ear and sent him sprawling.

Grump scrambled to his feet, scowling.

"Mind what you're doing, cotton head. Knocking a man about isn't fair. You didn't do it on purpose, did you?"

He glared at Herman suspiciously.

"Maybe you did. That's the trouble with you, I never can tell."

Herman whisked his trunk at the drum

hopefully, and shuffled his feet, but it was no use. The spell had been broken. Grump shook his head.

"No more games today," he said. "Anyway, it's stopped raining."

He was right. The sun shone now, and the earth was steaming. Herman looked towards the drum wistfully for a moment, then turned to go. Grump followed him to the doorway.

It was strange. Grump was sure that he disliked Herman, yet something was telling him to call the mammoth back. He didn't. Instead, he watched the great creature move slowly away. Only at the last moment did he call, but then it was too late. Herman saw his uplifted hand, but did not hear his shout. The mammoth wagged his head, and it seemed for a moment as if he smiled. Then he disappeared behind a hill.

"Good riddance!" Grump growled.

Even so, his face was sad as he turned back into his cave. That's when he heard a shout and children laughing. He turned to look out once more. Children were streaming across the ground towards his cave. His party guests were arriving!

Grump laughed. His party was going to take place after all.

9

Grump and the Tiger

"Buzz off, knobble knees! Can't you see we're busy?"

The group of cavemen glared at Grump as they stood talking outside their caves. Unlike the children, who were now Grump's friends, the other men still ignored him.

"It's not fair," he complained. "Just because they're in a bad mood they take it out on me. And all because of a silly old noise in the night."

Grump blinked blearily as he walked by the forest edge. He was very sleepy. That was the trouble, everybody was sleepy now. Every night for weeks they had been kept awake by a dreadful howling outside their caves, a hooting and groaning that had gone on and on. Grump shivered.

"Not that it worries me," he told himself bravely. "I don't believe in ghosts and suchlike."

Whooeeoooeeooo!

The noise came from right behind Grump, and with a shout of fear he leaped into the trees. He looked out, trembling, and his eyes widened in anger. It was Herman.

"Him again! Why must that great bottlehead always be playing tricks?"

Herman could certainly have picked a better day to play a joke on Grump. But he had no idea how scared the little caveman was just then of strange noises. He had hoped that a little tootling in his ear might cheer him up. It hadn't. Grump was gloomier than ever.

"Make a fool of me, would he?" Grump muttered. "Well, two can play at that game."

He followed Herman quietly through the forest. The mammoth was in no hurry. He sniffed happily at giant flowers, stirred a sleepy tortoise or two with his blunt grey foot, grunted with contentment. Life was so good. But at last he felt a little tired and looked for a cool spot to sleep. He saw a deserted cave in the hillside and trundled inside. Grump's chance had come.

"One good turn deserves another," he chuckled. "Must make sure old moth ears isn't disturbed."

Things couldn't have been better. A giant rock hung on the hillside over the entrance to the cave. A little digging, and the rock would come down and block the entrance. Herman would be trapped.

"And a good job, too. It'll take him all day to dig himself out. That will take the curl from his trunk." Grump got to work. Soon only a few pebbles held up the boulder.

"Can't reach them from here," he muttered. "Better try from below with a long stick."

That's how Grump came to be down by the cave entrance, probing with a long stick at the boulder. He was giving a last push with the stick when he felt a tap on his shoulder. He turned. Herman was beside him, his trunk raised once more to tap Grump, but on the head this time.

Grump didn't wait. He fled – right into the cave. At that moment the boulder crashed down and the cave entrance was blocked. Grump was in darkness.

"Dirty trick! Cheating big barrel!" he wailed. "I'll never get out of here!"

Grump didn't know that outside Herman was already digging to release him. Terrified, he groped his way through the darkness along the cave, seeking another way out. His hand touched something. He paused. His hand touched something again, warm and soft and gently moving. Grump recoiled in alarm. He wasn't alone in the cave. There was something with him, something alive. What's more, it had started making an eerie noise.

Whooeeooooeeooo!

Grump clapped his hands to his head in horror. The thing! The thing that had terrified everyone at nights with its wailing was here in the cave! He pressed against the rock wall and stared into the shadows. Where was it? What was it?

At that moment Herman managed to pull some rock from the doorway. Faint light came into the cave, and Grump's eyes opened as wide as dinner plates. He could see the animal now. It was a sabre-toothed tiger, and it was walking straight towards him.

"Go away! Shush! Go away and leave me alone!" Grump shouted, flapping his hands helplessly. No use. The tiger came closer.

Grump groaned and closed his eyes. There was nowhere to run. Soon he would be a tea-time snack for a hungry tiger. It came closer still and Grump's hair was blown back by its whining roar. Then the noise stopped. When at last Grump opened his eyes, he found the tiger seated before him. Its large green eyes seemed to plead with him. Grump took a nervous step backwards and frowned thought-fully.

"Strange, I've never seen a tiger with three front teeth before."

Grump was right. Where the tiger should have had two gleaming fangs there were three. Grump peered more closely, and the explana-tion was plain. A thin bone was caught behind the long front tooth of the tiger, and poked down like an extra fang. Grump jigged ex-citedly.

"Hurts you, does it? That's why you've been howling so much night after night. Like me to take it out for you?"

He reached forward very nervously. If he took out that bone, the tiger might make a meal of him afterwards. But he had to take that chance. Screwing up all his courage, he held the bone and pulled. He quaked as the tiger roared. Then suddenly the bone was free.

The tiger looked at the bone, at Grump, and back to the bone. Then it launched itself at Grump and crashed him to the ground. Grump clenched his eyes, sure that his last moment had come. But the tiger wasn't eating him. It was licking him, and making a noise that sounded very much like purring. Grump lay there in wonder.

Night had nearly fallen when Herman managed at last to roll the boulder from the cave entrance. He stepped back and waited anxiously. Soon Grump appeared, blinked solemnly at the setting sun, and walked away slowly.

Herman nodded in satisfaction. So long as the little caveman was safe, that was all he wanted.

Not long afterwards, the other cavemen saw Grump coming towards them. They nudged each other gleefully. They could never resist teasing him.

"You're out late, rock face," one of them shouted. "Careful the howling monster doesn't get you!"

"Not him!" called another. "His face would scare any monster away."

Grump glared, but said nothing. He usually let them joke until they were bored and left him alone. But tonight was to be different.

Suddenly an awful roar broke the evening. For a moment the cavemen stood transfixed in horror, then they turned around. Behind them, its fur standing on end and its jaws wide, was a sabre-toothed tiger.

They dived with shouts of fear behind some rocks. From there they watched in amazement as the tiger padded up to Grump and circled round him, rubbing against his legs. Grump did not move. He put his hand on the tiger's head, patted him fearlessly, and looked at the cavemen in triumph.

Long afterwards, when the cavemen were tempted to start teasing Grump again, they would remember that evening. For something else happened. Grump smiled!

He smiled as he looked down at the tiger, and for a moment he no longer seemed quite such an ugly little man after all. Then he turned, and, with the tiger padding beside him and Herman following in the shadows, he walked contentedly back towards his cave.